When The Blizzard Blows

Kenneth Jernigan
Editor

Large Type Edition

A KERNEL BOOK
published by
NATIONAL FEDERATION OF THE BLIND

Copyright © 1994 by the National Federation of the Blind

ISBN 0-9624122-9-5

All Rights Reserved

Printed in the United States of America

Table of Contents

Editor's Introduction

The Hook on the Doctor's Door . . 1

When the Blizzard Blows 13

From the Tricycle to the
    Cookie Jar 23

Love at First Sight 37

A Different View of the Grand
    Canyon 47

School and the Chicken
    House 53

Why Not Just Ask? 59

No Cane, No Dog! 71

The Verdict Is In 79

Kenneth Jernigan, President Emeritus
National Federation of the Blind

EDITOR'S INTRODUCTION

Now we are seven. This is the seventh Kernel Book, and the response to the series has been far better than we could possibly have hoped.

In previous volumes I have told you about meeting people on the streets, in supermarkets, in airports, and in all sorts of other places who have greeted me as a friend and told me of the pleasure and stimulation they have received from the Kernel Books. This continues to be the case—only more so.

A few weeks ago I was in Philadelphia attending a meeting. I was sitting in a restaurant before dinner when a man and woman (Walter and Gladys Gershenfeld, as I was to learn) approached my table and said, "Are you Kenneth Jernigan—the one who edits the Kernel Books—the one who wrote the article about standing on one foot?"

I told them that I was and they said that their whole family had been trying to see if they could stand on one foot for more than ten seconds. They were referring, of course, to my article in the sixth Kernel Book (*Standing On One Foot*) about a newspaperman who thought if you were blind you couldn't stand on one foot. They were not only having fun but also learning about blindness—learning that blind people are just like everybody else.

The present volume takes its title from an incident in the life of Marc Maurer, the able President of the National Federation of the Blind. When he was in law school in Indiana, he failed to take the initiative in helping an elderly woman and her three-year old grandson one winter afternoon during a blizzard. He didn't have much money, but that wasn't the reason. It was because he had not yet come to think of himself as a responsible person who should help others when the blizzard blows. Today he is both competent and confident and would not hesitate. The difference in his life has been the National Federation of the Blind.

So it is with me, and so it is with thousands of other blind people throughout the country. I hope this Kernel Book will give you a picture of who we are and how we see blindness—of what blindness is like, and what it isn't like. Above all, I hope it will help you to think of us as just ordinary people, people like you.

We laugh and cry, work and play, hope and dream—just like you. We also behave just like you when the blizzard blows—sometimes with courage, sometimes with fear, and often with a mixture of both. The selections in this volume are real life stories told by the blind people who lived them. I hope you will find them interesting and informative. I also hope they may be of at least some help when the blizzard blows.

Kenneth Jernigan
Baltimore, Maryland
1994

WHY LARGE TYPE?

The type size used in this book is 14 Point for two important reasons: One, because typesetting of 14 Point or larger complies with federal standards for the printing of materials for visually impaired readers, and we wanted to show you what type size is helpful for people with limited sight.

The second reason is that many of our friends and supporters have asked us to print our paperback books in 14 Point type so they too can easily read them. Many people with limited sight do not use Braille. We hope that by printing this book in a larger type than customary, many more people will be able to benefit from it.

THE HOOK ON THE DOCTOR'S DOOR

by Kenneth Jernigan

Not long ago when I went to a doctor's office for an examination, I had two or three things happen to me during the course of a few minutes that showed me how far we still have to come in changing public attitudes about blindness. In the examining room I was taking off my shirt and getting ready to hang it on a hook on the back of the door. I had my hand on the hook, so there was no question that I knew where it was.

The nurse said: "If I close the door, will you be able to find it?"

I don't know whether she was talking about the door or the hook, but it really doesn't matter. I had my hand on both of them, and the door was only going to move for a short distance.

There is no way that I could have lost it.

I later learned that the nurse had gone out to the waiting room and asked my secretary, who had come with me so that we could work while I was waiting, whether she wanted to come back and help me take my clothes off. That is not all. When I was leaving, the receptionist said to my secretary: "Does he need another appointment?"

What should I have done? How should I have reacted? What I <u>didn't</u> do was become upset or hostile. The nurse and the receptionist were well-intentioned and kindly disposed. They were doing the best they could to be of help to me. Moreover, if I am so touchy and insecure that I can be upset by people who are trying as best they can to give me assistance, then I had better look within. Confrontation was certainly not called for.

On the other hand, I shouldn't just leave the matter alone. I was pleasant and unperturbed, but I also took the occasion to talk about things I was doing and accomplishments blind persons were making. And I let the nurse see me tie my tie and find the door, trying to teach by example and not by sermon.

One thing that may have helped me keep my cool was an experience I had almost thirty years ago with a young blind fellow named Curtis Willoughby. He had just graduated from high school and was planning to go to college. He wanted to be an electrical engineer, and he didn't know whether a blind person could do it—and, particularly, whether he could do it. Of course, I didn't know whether he could do it either—but I hoped, put on a brave face, and did everything I could to encourage him.

Even though there were technical problems to overcome, he did extremely well in college. I continued to encourage him and talked now and again to his professors, assuring them that there would be no difficulty in a blind person's functioning as an electrical engineer. In reality they probably knew more about it than I did. Certainly they knew more about the technicalities of electrical engineering. But they seemed to need the reinforcement.

When Curtis graduated from college, I helped him make contacts and write job resumes. I talked to potential employers, assuring them that Curtis was competent and could do the work of an electrical engineer. I also continued to encourage Curtis and talked positively to everybody I met.

After about three months, Curtis was hired by Collins Radio of Cedar

Rapids, Iowa. He apparently did his work in a satisfactory manner since he received commendations.

A little while later, I was talking with a friend of mine who was a newspaper reporter, and he said to me: "Do you think Curtis is really pulling his weight at Collins, or do you think they are just keeping him for public relations purposes?"

I said, "I believe he is doing the job. I certainly hope so, but how can I be sure?"

The next spring another blind person graduated as an electrical engineer from Iowa State University, the same school from which Curtis had received his degree, and this blind person didn't have to wait three months for a job. He was hired immediately, and by Collins Radio. I hunted up my newspaper friend and said to him:

"I can now give you a firm answer. I think Curtis is pulling his weight at Collins for if they need one blind person for public relations purposes, they don't need two."

A few years went by, and Collins fell on hard times. They cut their work force by more than half and were in serious financial trouble. Engineers were laid off according to seniority, and when Curtis's number came up, he didn't ask for special privileges—which is the way it should have been. He took his layoff like the rest. We of the National Federation of the Blind don't try to have our cake and eat it too. We want equal opportunity, but we are also willing to make equal sacrifices and accept equal responsibility.

Anyway, Curtis took his layoff, and then he applied for a job as an electrical engineer with the telephone company. As director of programs for the blind in the state of Iowa, I had the responsibility of trying to help Curtis get another job. I thought he was a good electrical engineer, but I didn't know whether he was as good a salesman as I was. So I scheduled a lunch with top engineering officials at Northwestern Bell in Des Moines and talked about Curtis. I said he was a whiz at electrical engineering, and I did it with enthusiasm. They apparently believed me, for before we left the lunch, it was agreed that Curtis would go to work for the phone company.

He did, and after a time he was invited to spend a year at Bell Labs in New Jersey. This is a prestigious appointment, one that is only given to the best.

When Curtis finished at Bell Labs, he came back to Des Moines and resumed his work as a systems design engineer. One day without comment I received from Curtis a copy of a letter.

It was written by top engineering officials with AT&T, and it said something to this effect:

"Mr. Willoughby has been dealing with Problem X, and his work is some of the best we have seen. Please put this letter in his personnel file."

I called Curtis and said, "Tell me in two or three sentences what you did. If you make your explanation longer, I probably won't understand it."

As I remember it, he said that in large installations, such as manufacturing of farm equipment and the like, there were tremendous loads of electrical current and that these interfered with the phone system. There would be pixie effects—sometimes causing static and other interruptions and sometimes creating no problem at all. The filtering equipment necessary to remedy the problem was bulky and expensive. It would cost many tens of thousands of dollars if used widely throughout industry. Curtis had discovered a way to redesign the telephone system at these large installations so that the bulky filtering equipment would not be needed and another piece of equipment which had routinely been used could also be eliminated. The new design permitted more clarity in telephone conversations than would have occurred with the expensive filters or with the standard equipment.

After finishing this conversation with Curtis, I went into my office and literally locked the door. I sat at my desk and said to myself:

"You helped Curtis through college. You encouraged him in his search for employment. You did one of the best selling jobs in your life, convincing phone company officials that he could perform as well as anybody else as an electrical engineer. But deep down in your heart, have you ever really believed that he was fully, completely equal to a sighted electrical engineer?"

I wish I could say that my answer was an unequivocal yes. The truth is that I don't know. I had said it, and I had thought I believed it. But did I? After receiving the letter, I am certain that I did. But before that? I can't be sure.

This brings me back to the hook on the doctor's door. I have spent most of my life trying to convince blind people that they can compete on terms of equality with others, and trying to bring sighted people to the same belief. If under these circumstances I was still not certain that I believed in my heart that Curtis was pulling his weight, how can I possibly feel hostility, or blame others who fail to comprehend? What we need is compassion and understanding, not blame or bitterness. Although there are times when we must speak out and not equivocate, let me always remember the telephone company when I am annoyed by the hook on the doctor's door. I will fight if I must, but usually it won't be necessary—especially, if I remember Curtis and the phone company.

Marc Maurer, President
National Federation of the Blind

WHEN THE BLIZZARD BLOWS

by Marc Maurer

As Kernel Book readers know, Marc Maurer is President of the National Federation of the Blind. In this story he recounts with painful honesty an incident which helped to shape his character—an incident which helped prepare him to lead the National Federation of the Blind.

If a musician wants to become a virtuoso, it is necessary to practice. If an athlete wants to be a star, practice, practice, and more practice will be required. It seems to me that the simple but important things are often overlooked. When I think back, it seems to me that these simple things are often the most notable.

I like the winter months—especially when there is snow. The cold is stimulating, and the bite of the wind offers a challenge that requires preparation. One of the pleasures of the winter is stepping from a windy thoroughfare, after a long trudge through the snow, into a warm and steamy cafe for a cup of coffee. The gloves and hat come off, and the hands are grateful for the warm cup.

In 1976 I was a student attending law school in Indianapolis. I had begun college in 1970 and been married in 1973. Although I had been able to find some employment during the summer months, jobs (as is often the case with blind people) were hard to come by. My wife Patricia and I lived in a one-bedroom basement apartment on the west side of town four or five miles from the law school.

My wife, who is also blind, had been able to find employment (after a long, long search) as a typist for Blue Cross. Her checks paid the rent and bought some groceries, but there wasn't a lot of money left over at the end of the month. Our outings were infrequent and strictly rationed. Once we went to Wendy's for burgers. I remember eating two triples. I was very full but not the least bit sorry. Another time we went to dinner at Long John Silver's for fish and chips.

Each morning during the week, I would walk about a quarter of a mile from our apartment to the bus stop. After about a twenty-minute ride, the bus would drop me near the law school. Classes began about 9:00 o'clock in the morning. Sometimes they continued (with intermittent breaks) until late afternoon. But I was often finished with my formal work shortly after lunch. Then, there would be study in the library, or reading and writing back in the apartment.

At about two o'clock one afternoon, my classes had come to an end. I had heard on the radio that morning that there might be snow, and as I walked to the bus stop, I reflected that the weatherman had been right. There was already almost half a foot of it on the ground, and the stinging wet flakes were pouring from the sky—a veritable blizzard. The wind whipped the snow into my face and down my collar.

When I reached the bus stop, I discovered to my surprise that there were two other people waiting for the same bus. At that particular stop I was almost always alone. Today, however, a woman was waiting with her three-year-old grandson. Oh, but the wind was cold. Nevertheless, we talked about what a pleasant thing it would be to get inside out of the storm.

After a time the bus arrived. I climbed aboard, put my money in the fare box, and took my seat a couple of places behind the driver. The woman climbed aboard also with her little grandson. She explained to the driver that she was planning to travel the other way (east not west) but that it wasn't very far to the end of the line so she would ride out with us and come back.

The driver said that this would be all right, but she would have to pay two fares—one for going out and the other for coming back. The grandmother explained that she didn't have that much money with her. So the driver told her that she must get off the bus, walk one block over to the street on which buses returned toward town, and wait. With great reluctance and a little sadness, the woman and the child left the bus, and we started away from the bus stop.

Within a block I was wondering why I hadn't done anything to help. I wanted the grandmother and the little boy to be warm. I could have made it come true. But I sat without moving until the opportunity had passed. I looked in my pocket to see how much money I had with me, and I found two or three dollars. That would have been more than enough to cover the cost. I could have paid the fare myself, but I didn't. I let the driver put the woman and the child off the bus into the storm.

The recollection of that little boy and his grandmother are with me still. For almost twenty years I have been sorry that I did nothing to help. These two people symbolize for me the need to be prepared and to plan ahead to seize opportunities when they come. I could have made a difference to them that day, but I wasn't prepared to think in those terms.

If I want the world to be a generous place in which to live, I must begin with generosity in my own life. If I want (as indeed I do) strength of character, courage, gentleness, and the ability to face adversity, I must plan ahead to find ways to build these characteristics both in myself and in those I meet. Part of behaving well is the habit of thinking and acting in a certain way. All of this comes to mind when I remember a certain blizzard while I was waiting on a street corner for a bus.

When I was in Indiana, it was very unusual for a blind person to be attending law school. I was able to be there because my friends in the National Federation of the Blind had worked and planned in the years before I joined the organization to make it possible.

I needed books and a way to write that my professors could understand. I needed to know the techniques and skills that can be used by the blind to accomplish those things that would ordinarily be done with sight. I needed a background in traveling with a white cane. I needed the capacity to read and write in Braille.

I needed to know how to manage the ordinary activities of getting along on a daily basis—how to rent an apartment, how to acquire the use of a truck and a driver to move my belongings, how to manage a checking account, how to be sure that my neckties matched my other clothes, and how to locate people who would be willing to serve as readers—both for incidental matters like the mail and for those heavy law books. The National Federation of the Blind had helped me with all of this and had also assisted in finding the money to pay the tuition and other school fees.

But this is only a part of what the National Federation of the Blind provided. Far more important than all the other matters were the encouragement and support I received from my friends and colleagues in the Federation. What they said was, "You can do it; don't give up; keep trying; you'll make it!"

The law degree that is hanging on my wall would not be there if it had not been for the National Federation of the Blind. The planning and preparation which are responsible for that degree continue for thousands of other blind people throughout the nation. Do we want blind people to be independent and live successful lives? Of course we do. What must be done to create a climate of opportunity and to foster the kind of training which is needed? We must plan to build our programs with these objectives in mind. We want blind people to be a part of our society.

We want to help build our country so that we can be proud of what we have in America. That is why we have the National Federation of the Blind, and that is why I wish I had helped the woman on the bus.

Today I would certainly do it. Twenty years ago I didn't. Our road to freedom is a long one with many twists.

FROM THE TRICYCLE TO THE COOKIE JAR

by Barbara Pierce

What special problem does a blind parent face? You might guess a thousand times without coming up with the problem many blind parents consider toughest. Barbara Pierce has been blind from childhood and is the mother of three children, who are now adults. Here she writes about her efforts to overcome a particularly worrisome problem—the one you probably didn't guess.

All parents who take their responsibilities seriously are concerned about how to help their children grow up to be disciplined, honest, compassionate, and organized and to develop all the other virtues. But blind parents have one more responsibility: to keep their youngsters from absorbing the general public's poor attitudes about blindness and blind people.

My husband and I have raised three children, and in their formative years we tried hard to teach them that as their mother I was like other moms—helping with homework, fixing their favorite meals as birthday treats, and making them pick up their coats and books from the living room sofa. In our family there was always a division of labor: Dad drove and played catch; Mom baked cookies, bread, and apple pies. Dad trimmed hair and decided when fingers were infected; and Mom ironed clothes, sang songs, and sewed on buttons. Both of us listened to problems and helped to work out solutions.

Yet from the time the children were small, I knew that the world outside our happy home was lying in wait to complicate our lives. Evidence of this fact began piling up early and usually when I least expected it. I remember a day when Steven, our five-year-old, was at kindergarten. The baby had an appointment with the pediatrician, and I told Anne, then three, that she could ride her tricycle, which she had recently learned to pedal, to visit the doctor.

I put baby Margaret into her backpack, grabbed my long white cane, locked the front door, and prevented Anne from riding her tricycle down the seven steps of the front porch. Once we were safely on the sidewalk, we started the three-and-a-half-block expedition with Anne in front and me right behind, reminding her about stopping at the corner.

The first two streets we had to cross were very quiet, with cars seldom driving through the intersection, particularly in the early afternoon. Anne did well at the first crossing, stopping at the curb and waiting for my go-ahead before pedaling straight across to the other side. As we neared the second street, I dropped back a little to let her feel that she was making the decision of where to stop on her own. No cars were coming, so she was safe, and I was close enough to stop her if she decided to bolt for freedom.

She halted at the corner, and I was opening my mouth to praise her when I realized that an older man had materialized beside her and was bending down to talk earnestly to her. To my horror I heard him saying, "You must take very good care of your mommy because she needs your help."

I was humiliated to realize that he believed I was incapable of keeping my daughter safe, and furious that he presumed a sighted toddler was more competent than I to walk the streets of our small town. I made a brief comment to the effect that in our family the parents cared for the children and whisked Anne across the street. I have always been grateful that I did not recognize that neighbor, for it would have been hard in later years to be civil to him.

When we reached the other side, I asked Anne if she knew what the man had said to her. She shook her head vigorously and hopped off her bike to pick up a feather dropped by a passing bird. It was clearly more interesting to her than the conversation of an old man, and I was profoundly grateful.

The situation was a good deal different a few years later when our family visited a nearby amusement park. I rather like rides that swoop and twirl, and my husband absolutely does not. So I was the one designated to take the girls on the swings, a ride in which each person sits in a separate swing, is firmly strapped in, and then is whirled high into the sky for several minutes. We found three swings close together, and I made sure that each of the girls was strapped down before climbing into my own seat.

When we landed again, the attendant handed me back my cane, and I gathered up the girls and herded them down the exit ramp. When we reached the bottom, a woman hurried up to them and knelt down, fumbling with her purse. I asked her if there were some problem. And she explained rather hastily that she just wanted to give "these dear children some money," because she had been watching us, and she was so touched by the loving way they took care of me. She probably noticed my expression, for she quickly explained that they were so attractive and well behaved that she thought they deserved some reward for taking me on the rides.

I hurried the girls away, but they were unhappy. After all, that woman had been going to give them money, which was more than they could usually persuade me to do. I hardly knew what to say to them. Finally I explained that she had wanted to pay them for taking care of me; but that, since they didn't take care of me, it wasn't fair to take her money. They thought about that for a moment; then Anne summed the matter up with, "That's weird. Everybody knows that Moms take care of kids." I told her she was exactly right, and the lure of the roller coaster ended the conversation.

I was beginning to learn that, when I was around at the moment people did odd things because of my blindness or suggested to my children that I was not a proper mother, I could combat the problem. But I worried about what was happening to them when I was not present.

One day, when Steven was in fifth grade, he came home to say that he had had a fight on the playground because a kid had called him a liar when he described his mom's homemade pizza. (It's a recipe from northern Italy, given to me by a friend, and my family has always loved it.) But this boy said that a blind mom couldn't cook.

Another time Anne's teacher suggested that perhaps the room mother could supply cupcakes for Anne's birthday treat so that she wouldn't feel left out. Meanwhile Margy began sitting close to me when we watched television together in order to "explain what's happening." When I questioned her about why she had started doing this, she admitted that her friend's mother had told her that Margy's mommy couldn't understand "Sesame Street" unless Margy told her what was happening. I realized that something had to be done.

I went to the children's teachers and asked for a chance to talk to each of their classes about blindness. In Margy's class we played games that taught the children just how much they could tell about the world by listening and sniffing and feeling with their hands and feet.

They discovered that there are lots of ways to tell what's going on. I showed the older children how to read and write Braille and taught them how to offer assistance to a blind person who needs help crossing the street, and I explained how I crossed streets without any help. I brought homemade treats to all three classes and talked about how blind people cook and take care of their families.

That seemed to dispose of the negative comments from friends and teachers; but, as the children grew older, I became aware that they were increasingly disturbed by the way strangers stared at me when we were out in public. I should explain that, like many other competent blind people, I use my cane even when I am walking with a sighted person, so there are lots of opportunities for people to see me using my cane.

The youngsters began to resent the stares that I received, and they decided to take matters into their own hands. They thought the staring was rude, and they appointed themselves the official phalanx of stare-backers. They were prepared to stare down anyone who began staring at me as we passed. I tried explaining that these people had probably never seen a blind person using a white cane correctly and they did not know what to make of the situation.

But the kids agreed with each other: it was rude to stare at anyone; it was even more rude to stare at a person who did not know what you were doing. They believed they had a perfect right to call such rudeness to the attention of the person practicing it. Perhaps I should have protested and forbidden them to continue their campaign, but I decided that they needed to feel that they were doing something to counteract an activity they felt was inappropriate, unfair, and rude to me.

As the years passed, I continued to wonder from time to time whether the children's attitudes about blindness and me as a blind person had been negatively affected by the peculiar notions of other people. Then, when Anne was a junior in college, I received my answer.

A friend who teaches in elementary school had asked me to come speak about blindness to all the sixth grade classes in her school. I was happy to do so, and, because Anne happened to be at home at the time, I asked her to drive me to the nearby town where the school was located. At the close of my talk I asked if anyone had questions about what I had said. My daughter had been introduced, and one child asked her what it was like to have a blind mother.

Anne, who ran the citywide summer swimming program during college and had a way of making friends with youngsters, strolled to the front of the room and sat down on the edge of the teacher's desk beside me. She draped her arm across my shoulder and said quite seriously:

"It is really terrible having a blind mother! Do any of you have to do the dinner dishes sometimes?" A number of students groaned enthusiastically. "And does your mother expect you to clean up the kitchen too—I mean wiping off the counters, washing out the sink, and cleaning around the burners of the stove?" Again a chorus of agreement answered her. "Well, I discovered a long time ago that my friends only had to clean up enough to have things look okay. But, when you have a blind mother, you have to get things really clean because she doesn't inspect your work from the doorway; she comes in and touches everything. It has to *be* clean!

"And that's not all. Do any of you have cookie jars in your house?" A number said that they did. "We had one, too, and it was always full of cookies, which was nice for us when we could get at them. But we three kids learned when we were very little that, as long as Dad was the one watching us, we had a chance of sneaking cookies, if he wasn't looking. But when you have a blind mom, she hears the cookie jar lid no matter where she is in the house! It's terrible having a blind mother."

By this time they were all laughing with her and me. They had gotten Anne's message, that really life was no better and no worse with a blind parent, just a little different. And they were right.

I left the school smiling that day. My lovely, compassionate, talented daughter had demonstrated without even thinking much about it that she does know that blindness doesn't have to be a big deal. Together we had come a long way, from the tricycle to the cookie jar.

LOVE AT FIRST SIGHT

by Randy Rieland

The following story is reprinted from the October, 1993, issue of The Washingtonian. Besides being a delightful story of the Yeager family, it is a refreshingly positive example of the kind of news feature that helps rather than harms the public image of blindness.

Early on, Tracy knew that her parents' eyes didn't work.

Even at a few months of age, she realized that pointing at things brought no response. So Tracy, an infant testing life, found another way. She began grabbing her parents' hands and putting them on whatever she wanted. If she was hungry, she would touch her fingers to her mother's mouth. Together, Tracy and her parents, both blind since birth, began to shape their world.

Nancy, Jerry, and Tracy Yeager

Nancy and Jerry Yeager know all about pity. How to the sighted theirs seems a poignant world, rife with limitations. They know they will never see their daughter's smile, or watch her run across the room to them. But these images, they point out, are memories of the sighted. "If you don't see, what you aren't able to see of her is a non-issue," says Nancy.

It seems odd, then, to find a video camera on a tripod in the Yeagers' living room. To them, the camera makes perfect sense, even if, like most parents, they don't use it as much as they thought they would. "If we think she's doing something cute," says Jerry, "we aim the camera in the direction of the sound. It gives us an audio record."

Tracy's sounds are their baby snapshots, collected on tape or stored away in their memories, keepsakes of these times. "I love to hear her talking to herself in her bed," says her father.

Jerry, who's thirty-eight, had always worried about what kind of father he would be, because he didn't have much patience with babies. Nancy, forty-one, was nervous about how having a child would affect her career—she works for the Farm Credit Administration. "It was never an issue of 'Do we not want children because we can't see?' We knew we had both overcome enough obstacles. We knew we would deal with whatever came up."

They also had heard the stories from other blind parents of sighted children. Some people, the Yeagers were told, would think they had created a child to give them eyes. Others would feel sorry for Tracy, imagining a life dimmed by her parents' blindness.

Not long ago the Yeagers heard a woman tell Tracy, who had just turned two, "Now, honey, don't let your mom and dad get hurt." Nancy is particularly sensitive to the "poor blind person" treatment, no matter how well-intentioned, in front of her daughter. "We can teach her that blindness is okay. But when people act like we're helpless, what kind of message does that send to her about us?"

The Yeagers describe themselves as being like any other couple with a child. Little in their Alexandria high-rise apartment suggests otherwise. Toys lie scattered around the living room, flotsam from a toddler wave. "You learn to shuffle like this," says Jerry, sliding his feet along the carpet, "and kick them to the side."

A Barney tape sits ready next to the black-and-white TV. Nearby is a *Sesame Street* book—its Braille notations not only translate the words but also describe the images. At one end of the room is a red plastic table, crayons strewn across the top. It's the only place in the apartment where Tracy is allowed to color.

Nancy and Jerry always know where she is, but they don't always know what she's doing, and they don't want her wandering around the apartment with a crayon in her hand. Not that most parents wouldn't feel the same way, but the Yeagers, more than most, must set boundaries they can guard.

So they make rules, rules as ironclad as they are practical. Tracy knows, for instance, that she must answer when she's called. "Hide-and-seek is not a game we ever play," says Nancy.

Tracy also has learned to give her parents any strange object she finds. Once she handed them a wet caterpillar. "Our first thought was, 'Did she have this in her mouth?'" Jerry remembers thinking, "I figured, 'Well, she's gotten her caterpillar protein for the day.' "

"Daddy, can I run?" Tracy asks. She is standing outside the apartment door, looking down the long, narrow hallway that leads to the elevators. Jerry says okay and she's off, scrambling stiff-legged across the carpet. This is the one place where Tracy is allowed to run free, but even here there's a rule. Once the elevator bell rings, she has to grab one of her parents' hands and wait to get on with them. "She is a good little hand-holder," says her father.

The family tries to go out for a restaurant meal once a week. Just as often they go to the neighborhood playground, a trek that takes them through a parking lot and the sounds of moving cars.

Nancy and Jerry are used to maneuvering around traffic, but doing it with a two-year-old brings new risks.

So before they go out, they fit Tracy into a little harness. When it's secure around her waist, Tracy grabs the loose end of the tether and presses it into her mother's hand.

"When we go out," Nancy says, "we like to explore things together. I'll ask Tracy if she sees the birds that I hear. Or I'll ask her what color the flowers are that I smell. And if she asks me what something is and I don't know, I just tell her that I don't know. Sometimes we have to learn together."

What they have learned, above all, is that their lives are not about the disparity of blindness and sight, but rather how the two can merge. Sometimes Tracy will grab a cane and tap it in front of her. Sometimes Nancy will join in a game of mother-daughter peekaboo.

Tracy, across the room, crouches behind a playpen. Suddenly she pops up, giggling, "I see you, Mama."

"I see you, too," answers Nancy.

Nor does Jerry miss a beat a moment later when he is complimented on Tracy's grin.

"She has a beautiful smile," he says. "I just know."

Andrea exploring the Grand Canyon

A DIFFERENT VIEW OF THE GRAND CANYON

by Deborah Hartz

Deborah Hartz and her husband of Tucson, Arizona, decided that their daughter's blindness was not going to be a barrier to them or her in the enjoyment of a special vacation. They explained to skeptical friends that there were more ways than one to experience the Grand Canyon and that they intended to make the most of the opportunity to "see" it in a different way. Here is their story.

We stop to rest at the edge of the Tonto Plateau. Andrea tips back her canteen and drinks deeply. The water's hot from hours in the sun. Before her spreads the wide canyon.

Andrea listens. "I hear it. I hear the river."

Her baby sister, Laura, bounces in my backpack.

"Are you hot, Lolo? Here. I'll give you some water." Andrea finds the baby's mouth under the wide brim of the sun bonnet and tilts the canteen carefully.

"OK, Mom, I'm ready." Andrea reaches for my wrist, and we continue down the trail singing "Kookaburra." Soft dust puffs up around our feet with each step. Below us a sheer cliff drops away. Andrea is not bothered by the drop-off; she doesn't see it.

Andrea Barker, an experienced hiker, is blind. At the time of our Grand Canyon hike, Andrea was seven.

"That hike was neat because Grandpa and Uncle Myron hiked with us. My sister, Laura, was eight months old. She got to ride in Mom's backpack," Andrea recalls. "Pack it in, pack it out" says the trail sign. On that hike we had four days of dirty diapers to pack out.

Our hike began on the South Rim of the Grand Canyon. Because the South Kaibab trail is steep and deeply rutted, we often modified our guide technique. Andrea walked directly behind me and held onto the sleeping bag which was tied to the baby's pack. Movement of my pack gave Andrea a good idea of the trail ahead. A safety line connected the two of us.

The night before our hike the temperature on the rim had been close to freezing. It grew steadily hotter as we descended into the canyon.

"I was glad when we got to the tunnel," continued Andrea. "It was cool, and I've always loved echoes. The suspension bridge was fun, too. It swayed some, and our feet made neat noises as we crossed—like the Three Billy

Goats Gruff. The breeze from the river felt good."

The Bright Angel Campground at the bottom of the canyon was a welcome oasis. Water, large trees, flush toilets, picnic tables! A turkey wandered through the campsites ignoring the campers. Andrea was asleep before the tents were up.

In the morning, we walked to Phantom Ranch, where Andrea mailed a postcard to her teacher, written in Braille using a slate and stylus. Mail from Phantom Ranch is packed out of the canyon on mules. The lodge and restaurant at Phantom Ranch are supplied by pack mules.

We waded in the Colorado River and built sand castles before beginning the long hike out of the inner canyon.

On the trail we made up stories and songs to keep us going on the steep, uphill climb. One round was sung to the tune of "Three Blind Mice."

"Ringtailed cats, ringtailed cats. See how they run. See how they run. They run up the packbars to get in our packs. They eat all the fig bars that Grandpa has. Have you ever seen such a sight in your life as ringtailed cats, ringtailed cats."

Would she want to hike the Grand Canyon again? "Yes, definitely!" responds Andrea. "I'm in better shape now. It would be easier. When someone tells you how big the Grand Canyon is, you just can't understand it. You have to walk it yourself to really understand the size."

Dr. Homer Page

SCHOOL AND THE CHICKEN HOUSE

by Homer Page

Dr. Homer Page is Chairman of the Boulder County Board of Commissioners and a professor at the University of Colorado. He is also one of the leaders of the National Federation of the Blind of Colorado and of the national movement. Here he reflects on the things that helped him achieve success.

Miss Nellie Stice was my English teacher during my senior year at Buchannan High School in Troy, Missouri. She often read examinations to me. On the final examination I received 296 points out of a possible total of 300. When we finished the exam, she told me my score and said, "Have you ever thought about what you would be able to accomplish if you were not blind?"

Miss Stice did not believe blind persons could be successful. She believed that I had ability, and she felt badly that I, in her view, was destined to be thwarted in my efforts to use that ability. She genuinely felt pain for me. If any other of my classmates would have done so well (and none of them did) she would have said to that student, "Congratulations, you will go far in life," but those were not her expectations of me.

In spite of the withering message that I received from Miss Stice, I was generally encouraged as a child. When I was in the first grade, the teacher set up three groups of different learning levels. I was originally placed in the slowest group. My parents are not educated people. My mother completed the tenth grade, and my father went only to the eighth grade. However, they understood that it was not good for me to remain in that group.

They talked with the teacher, and I was moved up to the first group. I am sure that nothing my parents ever did for me apart from giving me life was so important to my future. If the teachers and administrators and other people had developed the expectations that I couldn't keep up with the demands of the school, then I hesitate to think what my life would have become. I am certain it would have been different and that it would have been much worse.

There was another time when my parents came to my rescue. During the summer between my third and fourth grades in school my family was visited by representatives from the Missouri School for the Blind. My father and I were on top of the chicken house putting down a new roof. We spoke with them from our lofty perch. They wanted me to attend the school for the blind in the fall. My father said no. He said, "My son is doing fine in school. I think a boy's place is with his family, and besides, who would help me with all this work if he were to go with you?" Few things could have been more important to a young blind child than to hear his father affirm that he was successful in school, loved and wanted by his family, and a productive contributing member of the economy of his family farm.

By the time Miss Stice made her comment it was already too late for my spirit to be damaged very much. I was on my way to college, and there were some things that I wanted to do. Now, decades later, I ask myself, "Have I been successful?" In some ways perhaps I have; but if I have, I haven't done it on my own.

I had a supportive family and generally helpful friends and teachers, and a group of people working for me about whom I had no knowledge until well into my adult life. That group was the men and women of the National Federation of the Blind. Even though I didn't know it, opportunities had been made available for me by the work of the generation of NFB members that preceded me.

*Doug and Peggy Elliott
December, 1993*

WHY NOT JUST ASK?

by Peggy Elliott

What is it like to be blind? A very reasonable question, but one which very often isn't asked. As Peggy Elliott points out here, how much easier it would be if it were.

Incidentally, for readers of previous Kernel Books, Peggy Elliott is the former Peggy Pinder. Here is what she has to say.

I've been blind for almost twenty-five years, and a lot of people have asked me, "What's it like to be blind?"

Often, the questioner has in mind some experience he or she had when the lights went out or when a blindfold was voluntarily worn for a few hours in one of those "trust walks" or "handicapped awareness days."

The problem is that those kinds of experiences give a false impression of what blindness is like. People wearing a blindfold for a few hours or losing the electricity are "temporarily blinded," just trying for a short period of time to fend until the ability to see returns. They haven't learned the techniques useful for doing things without sight. They haven't had any practice at it. And, their recollection is that blindness is pretty scary. Well, it is if you don't know how to handle it.

For me, learning how to handle blindness started when I met fellow blind people in the National Federation of the Blind. These were not only experienced blind people used to doing everything without looking, but they also were interested in passing along their knowledge and lots of encouragement with it. The day I met competent blind people eager to pass along their sense of confidence was the day I started really learning what it was like to be blind. Before that, I'd just been scared.

So, what is it really like to be blind? Three experiences I had while in college taught me a great deal about what it's like to be blind and what the blind person can do about it.

The first thing was that the college I attended imposed a physical education requirement for graduation—four semesters of it. I happen to be a wimp and hate exercise. Faced with wimpiness and the hurdle to graduate, one naturally starts thinking of ways around the hurdle. I did—or I did until my advisor contacted the college administration without my knowledge and presented me with the college's determination that physical education would be waived in my case. Now, *that* was the only way to get me to take a gym class and not complain about it.

The advisor and the administration both assumed that, because I was blind, I couldn't do physical activity and that I wouldn't want to be embarrassed by discussing it. So they worked out what they thought was a kindly way of taking care of the problem: I would be excused. I firmly told all involved that I wanted my college degree to have the same weight as all the other degrees that would be granted at the same time. If everyone else took physical education, then I would take it, too. I did it peaceably and without complaining.

That was my first lesson in what it's like to be blind: people around you in a genuine spirit of kindness think that you can't do things and are cheerfully willing to exempt you without even discussing the possibility that you can do it.

The second experience took place in preparation for a science lab.

Again, a science course with laboratory work was a graduation requirement. Now informed a little better about what might happen, I went to the professor teaching the class I had selected (geology) and asked to discuss my taking the class. He immediately said that the lab requirement could be waived.

I gave my reason for not wanting the requirement waived and then went on to say what I had prepared ahead of time. I told the professor that "he knew rocks" and that "I knew blindness." If we put our knowledge together and worked out ways of doing the lab so that I could learn the required material, I was sure that I could do the required lab and graduate with a degree equivalent to those of my classmates.

The professor thought about his knowing rocks and my knowing blindness for a long time. I patiently waited him out, knowing that this was a concept he needed to think about. Finally, he said: "That makes sense. Now, how shall we have you..." We talked details, worked out techniques, and I successfully took the course—a good one, by the way. It's interesting to learn how the world around you got the way it is.

Armed with my knowledge from these two incidents, I was not unready when the third one occurred. I was a philosophy major, and that department required a course on logic to complete the major. I registered for the course and completed the first section with a perfect score.

When the professor gave me my test score, he informed me that I would not be able to take the remainder of the course because there was a lot of work on the chalkboard throughout the rest of the semester. He preferred to teach without a textbook, using photocopied handouts and diagrams on the chalkboard instead—particularly the three interlocking circles called Venn diagrams. He stated that there was no way I could get the information, so I would have to drop the course.

I tried explaining that the course was required. He stated that the requirement would be waived. I tried explaining that I didn't want a waiver. He repeated his statement that I couldn't get the information and therefore couldn't pass the course.

Here once again, and in a very vigorous form, was the assumption that I could not do something. But this assumption threatened my major. And even more disturbing was the insistence on not discussing the issue with me. The professor simply stated what he thought and planned to make it stick. He thought he knew what blind people could do—and they couldn't read chalkboards. That was the end of the issue; and this from a professor of logic.

I decided that, in this case, I would not argue the matter at all. If someone was so certain that they knew what blind people could do, there was no point arguing. The only thing I could do was to show him. I told the professor I would be taking the rest of the class and, as politely as I could, walked away. There was no point in shouting or fussing. I'd just show him.

I was at a bit of a disadvantage in the conversation because I also had no idea how I was going to get the information. I just knew that I would. Every day, I took a piece of carbon paper to class and asked a classmate seated near me to make copies of the diagrams drawn on the board. As the classmate drew in his or her notebook, a copy was made for me.

I soon learned that this was unnecessary. The professor was such a plodding lecturer that, by the time he had finished drawing the diagram, he had actually described it about five times and explained it seven times more. You didn't need the diagram. But I had them anyway if I wanted to refer to them outside of class while using a sighted reader to explain how they looked.

I also learned that nobody else in the class was paying attention. The professor's style of lecturing was so dull and uninspiring that nobody listened. They just copied the diagrams and looked at them later. The diagrams by themselves told you nothing. You had to listen. So, people started coming to me in the dorm, asking me what the professor was talking about. I ended up tutoring many of my classmates since I seemed to be one of the very few who was actually paying attention.

When test time came around, I took the test and handed it to him. He scored it and informed me that I had scored 30 out of 100, noting as he told me that he had said I couldn't pass the course. I knew I had answered perfectly and insisted on going through the test, question by question. On the first question he had marked my answer wrong, the phrasing of the question itself permitted three possible answers. He had not noticed that and had only one answer in his test key. I explained that there were three possible answers. He grudgingly agreed and changed his test key.

There was still one question left, worth half the test. He had scored me wrong on that one, too. It was a memorized answer, based on the way he had drawn the diagrams on the chalkboard. He said I was wrong. I said I was right. I offered to go back to the dorm and get my carbon-copied notes to show him that he was remembering incorrectly the way he had drawn the diagram on the board. He very angrily pulled out his own lecture notes and looked at them for a very, very long time. Then he said: "Well, you're right." I didn't hear any more from him about not being able to do the work.

Not every denial of opportunity for a blind person works out so well. I did not know exactly how I was going to do the class work; I just knew I could find a way. But we often meet people like that philosophy professor who insist that we can't do something instead of people like the geology professor who are willing to discuss alternatives.

I don't mind being asked questions about what it's like to be blind and how I do things. The only thing I mind is when people assume that I can't do whatever it is. Sometimes, I want to say: Why Not Just Ask? I'll be glad to explain, and when I don't exactly know the answer, the National Federation of the Blind usually has someone in it who does.

So, what's it like being a blind person? It's like being any other kind of person.

NO CANE, NO DOG!

by Bill J. Isaacs

Today Bill Isaacs is a college professor and one of the leaders of the National Federation of the Blind of Illinois. Now he helps others understand that it is respectable to be blind. But it wasn't always like that. Here he tells of experiences he had before he began carrying a white cane to let others know that he had very limited sight. Bill now uses a guide dog.

I grew up with tunnel vision due to a congenital disease known as choroidoremia. The females are the carriers, while their male offspring are apt to become blind. I had a visual field of about three to five degrees (twenty degrees or less is classified as legally blind). I could see color; I could read a little, although I could see perhaps only four or five letters at a time.

On the farm I milked the cows; I worked in the garden; I hoed in the fields; I set tomatoes behind a planter; I even drove a Ford tractor with the wide front wheels, with which I plowed and cultivated.

Then, after graduating from high school, I went off to the big city, where I attended a business college for twelve months. Following the completion of my work at this college, I worked in a private warehouse office for a couple of years before taking a Civil Service exam, which led to a job in the U.S. Treasury Department, where I served as a claims examiner for corrections on income tax returns.

I was in my early twenties before I was even aware that I was legally blind. It's one thing to know that you are legally blind, but it's quite another thing to come to terms with it. I knew I had poor vision and saw virtually nothing after dark. I grew up in a small, quiet, rural community amidst a family of sixteen children, where nearly everybody in the county knew some member of the family. I never felt blind. I was usually with some member of the family, for everybody else around understood my situation better than I did myself.

Later, however, things were different. I faced new situations in the big city, where people didn't know me and I did not understand my own limitations. Later still, seven years after having graduated from high school, I enrolled in an out-of-state college to prepare to become a history teacher. That is when the bombshell really hit me.

I found myself surrounded by numerous strangers and a new environment which I did not know. It was not too difficult at first since my younger brother came to college and shared my dorm room, but after about six weeks because of both homesickness and lovesickness, he returned home and got a job and was soon married. Mind you, I never used a cane, wore dark glasses, or even dreamed of using a guide dog. I told no one that I was blind.

I got myself into awkward positions in crowded stairways and hallways. My limited vision did not adjust well from a bright, sunny day to the darkness of a building interior. I could not read room numbers identifying classrooms. I found it embarrassing and difficult to participate in activities after dusk. Games involving motion (such as football or playing tag) were out for me.

The real shocker came one day when a veteran student, who had suffered torture in a Chinese prison camp during the Korean War, rather bluntly made the following remarks to me:

"Bill, why do you come walking into the classroom each day as if you were the king of the walk? You never greet anyone. You march to the front of the room and across the front to the window side without acknowledging anyone."

I had to stop and analyze that comment a bit. I had to admit that what he said was true. I nearly always sat in the front row by the window side to get the maximum amount of light so I could see to take notes. When my body is in motion, such as walking, I have to concentrate all my powers on the small little patch that I see for mobility purposes.

Consequently, I did not see anyone—or if I did, it was only a small portion of their body, which was an obstacle to be bypassed. I think you can begin to see the picture here. The white cane would have been a silent answer to many questions. Out of my frustrations I went to my English professor, with whom I had developed friendly relations.

She encouraged me to talk about my problem as part of my speech requirement in that class. I did that toward the end of my first semester. Immediately thereafter, as news spread by word of mouth to other students and faculty members, my isolation and feeling of blindness evaporated.

Whether I was at the college, on a bus, or at a terminal, students and faculty alike understood my situation and often offered their services to help when they thought I needed them. Of course, that sort of thing can be overdone at times, but it can also be rather comforting to know that they know you are blind.

As I look back I realize how much easier it would have been if I had carried a white cane to let people know I was blind. I think particularly of an incident when I was working at the U.S. Treasury Department. In this job I rode in a car pool, where I was picked up at a busy downtown intersection. One Friday night when I thought everybody else was staying in town, a car pulled up and parked, and I opened the door to enter. Just before getting into the car, I heard a lady running up behind me towards the car, so I let her get in first. Then I got in.

After driving two or three blocks, the driver said, "Are you going to go to the bank with us?" As soon as he spoke, I knew he was not my driver. The lady thought I was with the driver, the driver thought I was with his wife, and I had embarrassingly to get out of the car at another busy intersection and get back to my place in a hurry—and with considerable difficulty. The white cane would have been the answer.

I finally started using the white cane about twenty years after I should have started with it, and now I wonder why I was so foolish or so ill-informed about it. If one has restricted vision, the general sighted public considers you blind whether you are or not. The white cane is not only a silent "answering symbol" that goes straight to the point, but it is a very useful piece of equipment. It does, as it were, extend your fingers all the way to the ground. It picks up many messages and relays them back to you better than the shuffling of your feet or the trailing of your fingers.

Of course, you will have some embarrassment when you first attempt to use a cane, but after two or three weeks of continual use, picking up the cane becomes as routine as brushing your teeth or putting on your glasses.

THE VERDICT IS IN

by William D. Meeker

Bill Meeker is the President of the Milwaukee chapter of the National Federation of the Blind of Wisconsin. He is also a conscientious citizen with a wry sense of humor and a conviction that, if he is to insist on receiving the rights of first-class citizenship, it is also his duty to carry out its responsibilities. Here is how he tells it:

Who, me—the one who never wins anything except an occasional $1 scratch-off lottery prize or an opportunity to buy some choice property accessible only to helicopters and mosquitoes—summoned to jury duty? Impossible! Someone must be suing me instead, or else this is a newer and more cleverly packaged real estate scam. I'd better read that summons again more closely. But no, I am to be a reserve juror. I am instructed to call the Milwaukee County Courthouse Jury Management Office to see if I am needed. What if I'm actually picked to serve? I feel excitement and fear simultaneously.

Co-workers and friends rallied to support me. "Don't worry, you don't stand a chance. You're a federal employee. They don't pick federal employees." "They won't pick you. They rejected me twice after I told them I was a musician. The whole experience was pretty boring, but the hot chocolate was great."

But I am not a musician. Interestingly, none of my friends mentioned my blindness as a possible reason for rejection. None of us had considered two pivotal factors: First, potential jurors will go to almost any extremes of whining, crying, preposterous excuses, and grovelings to avoid jury service. Second, at the time of my adventure jury selection was underway in the trial of a Cedarburg man for the brutal and highly publicized murder of his wife.

So I was needed, and I did report to the auditorium-like jury assembly room just in time, as it turned out, to catch the last half of the exciting western movie, *Hangman's Knot*, on the wide screen TV. From time to time the overhead loudspeaker blared my name along with a number (usually above twenty-five) which corresponded to a number painted on the floor on which I was to stand—so far, nothing exceeding my intellectual capabilities.

Having found my numbered spot by using my eight-plus years of parochial school training in "forming an orderly line," I visited a number of courtrooms, listened to a variety of questions from lawyers and judges, and heard an amazing array of preposterous, whining, groveling excuses for why these potential jurors were unable to serve. It was a humbling experience to see otherwise ordinary people displaying a level of creativity normally reserved for writers of fantasy.

In a civil courtroom on my second day of call and wait and march in line, a sufficient number of people ahead of me had presented creative enough excuses to be released from jury service that it became my turn to sit in the jury box and be questioned by the attorneys. When I rose from the general seating to approach the jury box, opposing counsels rocketed from their seats to intercept and escort me around the videotape player (present to play a recorded deposition) into the jury box. To my surprise, not a single question about my blindness was asked, and when the final jury selection was made, I was among those selected.

The trial, a trumped-up defamation of character suit, lasted two days. Seeing me using my Braille 'n Speak, the judge asked if I was taking notes and answered "good" in a tone which made me think that he wished more of my fellow jurors would do likewise when I said that I was.

My fellow jurors exhibited one piece of noteworthy behavior: When the time came to be marched from the jury room into the courtroom each day and after breaks and lunch, they all hung back deferentially to allow me to lead the procession into the jury box. But when court recessed for breaks, lunch, and the evening, they stampeded off, not caring if I was first or last. Well, "When the going gets tough,...."

After rendering our verdict on the third day, we were thanked for our service and assured that we would not be called again for at least two years. Too bad, I enjoyed serving. Also I enjoyed the attention that was *not* paid to my blindness. Ladies and gentlemen: the jury has reached a verdict: there is justice for blind people in the Milwaukee County court system.

You can help us spread the word...

...about our Braille Readers Are Leaders contest for blind schoolchildren, a project which encourages blind children to achieve literacy through Braille.

...about our scholarships for deserving blind college students.

...about Job Opportunities for the Blind, a program that matches capable blind people with employers who need their skills.

...about where to turn for accurate information about blindness and the abilities of the blind.

Most importantly, you can help us by sharing what you've learned about blindness in these pages with your family and friends. If you know anyone who needs assistance with the problems of blindness, please write:

Marc Maurer, President
National Federation of the Blind
1800 Johnson Street, Suite 300
Baltimore, Maryland 21230-4998

Other Ways You Can Help the National Federation of the Blind

Write to us for tax saving information on bequests and planned giving programs.

or

Include the following language in your will:

"I give, devise, and bequeath unto National Federation of the Blind, 1800 Johnson Street, Suite 300, Baltimore, Maryland 21230, a District of Columbia nonprofit corporation, the sum of $___ (or "___ percent of my net estate") to be used for its worthy purposes on behalf of blind persons."

Your contributions are tax deductible